PEDAL ZOMBIES

PEDAL ZOMBIES

THIRTEEN FEMINIST BICYCLE SCIENCE FICTION STORIES

EDITED BY

ELLY BLUE

EBP

PEDAL ZOMBIES
THIRTEEN FEMINIST BICYCLE SCIENCE FICTION STORIES

Edited by Elly Blue

First printing, September 15, 2015

Made in the USA

ISBN 978-1-62106-562-3

Find more feminist bicycle science fiction and many other titles at ellybluepublishing.com

Microcosm Publishing
2752 N Williams Ave.
Portland, OR 97227
TakingTheLane.com
MicrocosmPublishing.com

Cover art by Amelia Greenhall | AmeliaGreenhall.com

This is the third volume in the *Bikes in Space* series

To find other volumes, or to submit your own feminist bicycle science fiction stories, go to bikesinspace.com

[Table of Contents]

INTRODUCTION · 6

NOTES ON ZOMBIE SPECIAL EDITION CATALOG by Jessie Kwak · 12

RIDING THE CIRC by Jim Warrenfeltz · 21

ON EACH OTHER'S TEAM by T.M. Tomilson · 33

THE LONG WAR by Bob Simms · 41

THE BREEDERS by Emily June Street · 49

THE BIKING DEAD by Maddy Spencer · 69

PEDALING SQUARE by David J. Fielding · 77

INTERCHANGE by Ellie Poley · 85

DEADMONTON by Alexandrea Flynn · 98

DEAD ROCK SEVEN by Cat Caperello · 111

NIGHT OF THE LIVING CARS by Elly Blue · 120

WHY I RIDE by Gretchin Lair · 136

BICYCLE SCIENCE FICTION REVIEWS by Aaron M. Wilson · 141

CONTRIBUTORS · 151

INTRODUCTION

In April, 2011, I started to panic on the BART. For the ten-minute trip under the San Francisco Bay, each person in my range of vision was looking down at their phone, completely silent and absorbed.

I had a headache, and the changing pressure as we sped under the bay was making it worse. I forced myself to look over my shoulder at the staggeringly normal view of an old man napping and a young woman writing in a notebook.

When I looked back straight ahead, the scene was unchanged. But slowly it shifted. The man seated across from us abruptly put his phone in his pocket and began to pray. The guy with the skateboard on the other side of the doors stood up, and I saw that he had been hunched over a paperback book the entire time.

Then we came to the West Oakland stop and things started moving again.

That night, and ever since, I haven't been able to stop thinking about zombies.

Before this, I'd never been remotely interested. *Shaun of the Dead* was a funny, timely parable, but the gore and kitsch and Jane Austen mashups never appealed to me. But I started to read and to ask around, and what I found was much more complicated and interesting than expected.

The original zombie stories were powerful tales of witchcraft and colonial control of peoples' bodies. In the last decade, it's the colonizers who have become obsessed with zombie stories, and we have given them new, disturbing meanings. Sometimes they seem to be violent, unthoughtful parables of some sort of class or racial division gone very wrong. Other times, they read like true stories of city life, where a chronically unhealthy, lonely population slogs through their days behind the wheel of a car, while looking at their phones, mistrustful of anyone who hasn't gotten the virus; the special, individualistic unbitten meanwhile hail each other as heroes, high-fiving and cracking jokes as they wreak casual destruction on everyone else. And of course these stories increasingly tap into anxiety about end of the world.

It was on that same trip in 2011 that, riding down Market Street in Oakland, we saw the giant orange billboard predicting the end of the world coming up that May 27th. We laughed about it a few times and then I forgot about it until it was suddenly all anyone was talking about on Facebook. The millennial feeling was contagious. It took some effort, for a few days, not to crack a joke about the end times, or to click "like" on the fan page for stealing everyone's stuff after the Rapture. Of course, it's easy to laugh at a wingnut predicting the end of the world, when the daily news is far more dire.

Perhaps by ironically performing the events that scare us to an exaggerated degree we can soothe our real fears. Zombie marches happen at least once a year in Portland. The idea is that dozens or hundreds of people dress as zombies, with elaborate makeup and ripped clothes, and march through the streets staring vacantly and jerking their arms around. Sometimes it's a bike ride; often it culminates in a zombie prom or other kind of zombie party. Alcohol is a factor.

My friend April has been participating in these since 2006. I asked her: Why? Why do all these people want to be zombies, rather than, say, heroic zombie hunters?

"The makeup is really easy to do," she said. "And it's fun."

Pressed further, she divulged that the friend who got her into the zombie scene "definitely felt like the world was turning him into a zombie."

And finally, "Zombies are scary because *people* are scary."

We are scary. Whether we're more terrifying to ourselves or each other is an open question, but it's obvious to anyone who's been going to the movies lately that we are telling a lot of scary stories about the future of humanity. Zombie stories are by nature dystopian. Zombies signify failure—of political will and social cohesion, of technology and medicine, of the human body and soul. These are all topics that are being battled over right now, among people who care about all three worlds that this series occupies: science fiction, feminism, and bicycling. Questions permeate news and Internet discussions like: Who has power and who ought to? What forms of social or personal control are desirable and which are anathema? What is the line between life and death, humanity and inhumanity? When it comes down to it, who will survive?

Welcome to the third annual Bikes in Space. These stories may not answer every question you have about the future of humanity, but I hope they at least entertain you along the way.

Elly Blue
Portland, Oregon
June, 2015

NOTES ON ZOMBIE SPECIAL EDITION CATALOG

Jessie Kwak

From: Joanna Ecco

To: Creative Team

Re: Notes on Fall 1 Catalog

So far so good, people. Thanks for staying focused, I know it's been difficult with what's going on in the news. Also, has Tania checked in with anyone? Merchandising wants to add new product. This is not a good time for our photographer to be AWOL.

- **Raul** - I need to see finalized images by Wednesday. Consensus from Sales is to lose the blood spatters. Can you clone those out? Please tell me we don't need to reshoot.
- **Martina** - Enough with the *Night of the Living Dead* references in the product copy. Puns don't sell bikes. Specs sell bikes.
- **Steph** - Come by my office, let's go over cover options. Do we have any shots of the model where she's showing more muscle?

And Sales isn't into the shotgun poses, they say it confuses customers. We're a bike catalog, not a small arms dealer.

ADDED SKUs:

- SKUs #41217 & #41218: We FINALLY got the sample product for the new Gore ZombieProof® Active Shell Jacket and Pants. **Martina**, product specs are on the Creative drive. Play up the bite-deterrent-yet-stylish stuff in copy, but Legal says don't make too many promises. **Steph**, shooting laydowns of these is priority one for Tania when she gets in. They're going on the commuter spread (44/45).
- SKU #43189: XLC LazerBlade® Mini U-Lock. **Steph**, hi-res image is on the Creative drive. **Martina**, emphasize the safety features on this, we don't want people thinking the lasers will turn on in their back pocket anymore. XLC swears they've worked out that bug.

DROPPING SKUs:

- The Bay Area has gone dark, so Merchandising doesn't think we can get any more Clif Bar product. Drop all carry forward Clif SKUs on the nutrition spread (32/33). Merch will turn over replacement items later this afternoon. Remaining Clif Bars will be stockpiled in the warehouse, but the news keeps saying it won't come to that around here, so no worries.

This is the approved copy for Model ZA-11 Ranger and the Model ZAP-13 UltraVolt:

RANGER: This tough-riding, indestructible commuter will get you through the Apocalypse. Hands down the most hassle-free bike on the market, with an ultra-silent Gates Carbon Belt Drive and low-maintenance Shimano Alfine Internal 11-speed rear hub. Comes standard with our patented indestructible titanium-zombonium® alloy disc brakes. Face the Apocalypse head on when you add the optional collapsible gun rack and double Uzi holster. Steel. Colors: Lava, Espresso.

> ULTRAVOLT: Endurance race geometry combines with the latest in long range electroshock weaponry for a high-voltage, high-adrenaline off-road bike. 27.5" wheels handle any obstacle they come across —as does the quick-fire VeNom® system. The 275-volt piezo-electric projectiles stun instantly, and with a range of 30 meters and up to 25 charges, *you'll* be the menace of your local trail system. Aluminum. Colors: Citrus, Aqua.

Martina – Do we need to mention that Uzis aren't included with the Ranger? Sales is concerned. Lowest common denominator and all that. And I know you hate "zombonium." I know it's probably just the same alloy we've always used. But R&D says it's a thing, so we use it in copy. End of story.

Raul – The graphics on the ZAP-13 need to really sizzle. Can you bring out the greens and yellows? Also, any way to show the stun gun thing in action? Questions? I'll be in my office.

Thanks,

Joanna

#

From: Joanna Ecco

To: Creative Team

Re: Re: Notes on Fall 1 Catalog

- **Steph** – I talked to Kelvin in the warehouse about helping out in the photography studio since Tania hasn't checked in. Kid has an art degree, so he can probably figure out how to work a camera. Also, can you forward a press kit to that reporter from BRAIN?
- **Raul** – The retouched ZAP-13 graphics are perfect, thanks. Unfortunately, Production just told me they're changing them. See attached file. Can we clone those in? No time to reshoot.
- **Martina** – "Great minds taste alike"? When I said no *Night of the Living Dead* references, I also meant no references to *Walking Dead* or *World War Z* or any zombie puns AT ALL. It should go without saying that the headline for the components spread (48/49) will not be "Chaaaaaiiiinns." Keep it classy. We're in

an apocalypse, people are dying. Don't make me give you a list of outlawed words.

ADDED SKUs:

- SKU #48990: PDW BlueDiamond Taillight. **Steph**, Merchandising should have a hi-res image to you by this afternoon. **Martina**, Apparently it's a thing that they can't see the color blue. Roll with it. PDW has a FAQ page on their website with all the specs. Again, Legal says not to make any promises. Goes on electronics spread (46/47).

DROPPING SKUs:

- ALL BELLS. Sending a separate email with specific info, but FYI, apparently they really go crazy when they hear bells. Bells are out, going forward. **Steph**, come by my office and we'll discuss other options for the accessories page.
- SKU #43189: XLC LazerBlade® Mini U-Lock.

Steph and Raul – I sent you a meeting request. We need to talk about prAna's camouflage line. Do we have any other images from that shoot? I want the model to look more serene, but still wary. And the katana is overkill. Clone it out.

If you haven't heard the news, there is now a contagion alert for the whole metro area. They're recommending that we all stay put, so the guys in the warehouse are sorting out sleeping and food arrangements. Talk to Operations if you have any questions, and pass the message on to your families.

Thanks,
Joanna

#

From: Joanna Ecco

To: Creative Team

Re: Re: Re: Notes on Fall 1 Catalog

This catalog is going to the printers on Saturday. This is a hard deadline, people. I expect to see all-nighters. And it's not like any of us have homes to get back to anyway.

- **Everyone** – If you see Tania DO NOT LET HER INTO THE BUILDING. Come see me if you have any questions.

ADDED SKUs:

- SKU #49181: Burley BearCub Armored Baby Trailer. Going on the kids spread (16/17). Merchandising is working on getting hi-res images, but it sounds like things are getting tough in Eugene right now. **Steph**, can you find room in the spread? We can drop the Trail SnakPaks if we need space. **Martina**, we don't have any product sheets. I'm sure you can find everything you need for copy on Burley's website.

- **Steph and Martina** – Merchandising will be doing drive-by turnovers today to fill holes in the accessories spread (24/25). A handlebar-mounted motion sensor that CatEye just released, and couple handguns to cross sell with the Detours saddlebag holster. Turns out we're a small arms dealer after all. **Steph**, can we get these to Kelvin to shoot ASAP? **Martina**, Google the specs.
- SKU #43189: XLC LazerBlade® Mini U-Lock.
- (Online only) SKU #49908: Stainless Steel Katana. Will turnover this afternoon. This is the same katana from the prAna shoot. Sales thinks it's a good cross sell. **Raul**, can you add that back into the photos? Also, we just got the camouflage shipment, and the production colors are all completely different than the samples they sent us. You'll need to color correct. Merchandising will bring them by. **Martina**, this is online copy only, please add "katana available online" to the copy block for SKU #43353

(prAna Inner Strength Bulletproof Camisole).

DROPPING SKUs:

- SKUs #41217 & #41218: Gore ZombieProof items DO NOT WORK. Turns out they've been losing testers over there. Please replace with SKU #38990 Showers Pass Zombies Pass FlakJacket - pick up the copy and images from Summer 2.

Dinner's at 6 tonight, R&D is cooking spaghetti. Creative is excused from cooking shifts until all pages release to the printer. Attendance at weapons training demos is still required - next one is at 4:30 in the break room.

Back to work, people. We have a catalog to print.

Thanks,

Joanna

RIDING THE CIRC

Jim Warrenfeltz

"You don't drop anyone while you're in the city. No matter what happens. No matter what you see. No matter who, or what, is after you. You don't drop *anyone* while you're in the city."

I looked around at my fellow riders. We were all nodding, dutiful little students to the teacher. Yes, we all agreed, we are a team. We work as one. One for all, and all for one, and all that hokey stuff from the kidvids. Spirit of the Twenties! Together, we survive!

Never bought into it myself, and somehow I didn't think that the collection of misfits around me did, either. Take this scathead kid, Rorie, that I picked up coming up the Garden State. Found Rorie on the side of the road, trying to fix a flat while keeping eyes on all the rusty remnants. Pure paranoia. No one dead had walked out of those things for five, ten years.

“First time out of the village walls, kid?” I said, downshifting and kicking free of the pedals. Always good to announce yourself vocally. Some people can get anxious, even when you’re on a bike. Zombies don’t ride bikes, but try telling that to someone who just blew your head off. You can’t. You don’t have a head.

“Kid yourself. I’m Rorie. Rorie Fontaine?” The kid meant for it to be a statement that carried an impact, but the inflection at the end turned it into a question, a question that told me exactly who this Rorie Fontaine was supposed to be. Rorie was a top shit racer in a small town. Rorie might have posted a few helmetcam vids online. Maybe one had even hit a few thousand views. Probably had a few fans amongst the local brats.

“You never heard of me?”

If you have to ask, kid... “Look, I can spot for you for a few minutes. Get you back in the saddle. Then I gotta get going to this thing—“

"The Circ?" A gleam in the dawn light as Rorie's teeth flashed. Could have been a smile. Could have been a challenge.

I nodded, slowly. "Yeah. The Circ."

"Great. You can come with, that's where I'm headed."

I rode sweep while Rorie led the way. Amazingly, Rorie seemed to be one of the more put-together Circrider aspirants on the Weehauken field. Glancing past Rorie's green mohawk, I saw many young, angry, and pimply riders, a couple who were clearly stoned, and one who didn't even have a pack. Don't know where they thought they were going to pick up a spare tube in Old Newyork. S'pose you could just ask the zombies, real nice-like.

"Alright then, here's the plan." I looked back at the Circ Ride organizer. A row of studs up each ear and steely blue eyes that inspired confidence among the young and easily led; calves chiseled out of solid oak that inspired confidence in me. "We walk our bikes through the Lincoln Tunnel. It's too jammed to ride, but if we stay on the catwalks, we'll be fine. Any roamers in there were put down years ago. Single file, everyone stay in contact, no one panic. Nobody afraid of the dark, right?" Nervous laughs all around.

"After that, we get out, we go south. Keep the water on the right the whole ride. We keep pace, we keep *moving*. I want us rounding the southern tip in fifteen minutes, midway up FDR in thirty. Follow the line of the person in front of you. We round the top of the island in less than an hour, we're doing good. Then it's a straight shot down the Westside Expressway, back into the tunnel, we walk our bikes out, we're back here in an hour and a half. Quick and painless.

"A few rules. We do *not* drop anyone in the city. We do *not* go into the heart of the city. If you get into serious trouble, you ditch your bike and you *swim*. That is why we stay by the water. It's the

Circumference Ride, not the Circ-and-a-bit-in-the-middle Ride. Swimming is safe.

"What we are doing is *illegal*. But we're going to move fast, be in and out quick. The policebots won't have time to tag us. And hopefully none of you is dumb enough to be carrying or wearing anything identifying." The leader glanced doubtfully at Rorie's green spikes.

One of the pimply, angry kids spoke up. "Hey, I heard that, like—they're cracking down on stuff hard, right?"

The leader speared the kid a glare. "Maybe. I heard the same thing. Some people I know might not be on the streets anymore. Things are getting a little thin. If you want to drop, though, drop now. Go home now. The rest of us are doing this."

The kid dropped their eyes. The leader continued, "If you see a zombie, call it out. Keep the pace. Have a good ride. And *no one* gets dropped in the city."

We all nodded again, dutifully. For such iconoclasts and rugged individualists, we were easily bossed around by someone with a strong voice and piercing eyes. And great calves.

"I'm pulling. And..." the leader scanned the crowd, once, twice. Settled on me. "And I'm going to put you as sweeper, alright?"

"Alright." Why do I have to be so competent-seeming?

There wasn't much to say after that. We scooted down the ramp into the tunnel, skirted the barricades and the signs spelling out the penalty for what we were doing, and were underground.
The walk through the tunnel wasn't so bad. Dark, sure. Rustling sounds, of course. Could have been rats. I was glad to see the sun again on the other side.

We mounted up and were on the east side drive before we saw our first zombie. Just a shuffler, trapped in one of those fenced-off hundred square feet of green the Old Nukers had called parks. But the groan got us going, and we made good time the next few miles for sure.

Coming 'round the top of the island twenty miles later, the initial surge of adrenaline was long gone, the kick of breaking the law was wearing off, and the Circ Ride was beginning to feel like a bust. We had seen a few more zombs, sure, and the big buildings were amazing, but the view begins to wear on you. I don't know what I was expecting.

Ruminating on these thoughts, I didn't shout out when Rorie broke from the peloton ten miles on. I simply followed, leaving the group and heading into the heart of the city.

A couple of short blocks later, weaving through the rusted, tangled, burnt-out hulks, our speed way down, on the cleared-out Westside Expressway (which, I have to admit, felt a little tamed—almost touristy and dilettante), I called out to Rorie, low and quiet, but loud enough to carry over the wind and sound of our wheels, "Where you headed?"

Rorie tossed a look over their shoulder, nodding at me. "You didn't want that kiddie stuff, right? Damned if I ride in Old Nick without seeing The Loop."

The Loop in the Park. A 10k dream ride that old-timers still talk about. In a city of millions that had once meant thousands of bikers at any time, looping through the hills and trees. A biking mecca. And, of course, as the talk had it, now swarming with zombies. Not to mention open to the policebots, being unshielded from sat coverage. But still. The Loop.

"Let's do it," I said, the words spilling out of my lips before my brain formed them, pure spinal cord response.

We rode it. The whole thing. And it was glorious. Roads without rusty hulks blocking them. Zombies by the score, but too slow and sleepy in the morning sun to keep up with our pace. Blasting down one side of a hill, burning up the other, legs pumping, pumping, pumping, laughing in the morning light and veering to one side to hit a zombie with your tire pump just because you can.

But then there was the droning whine. Behind and to the left, then another behind and to the right, interfering with each other's sounds waves and making a dreadful, throbbing, high-pitched buzz. Policebots.

You don't look at a policebot. You keep your retinas to yourself. But when a shadow falls over you as you ride, you can't help it, you turn your head toward it. Instinct from when we were little monkeys and feared the piercing grip of the talons. What's old is new again.

I looked up, I admit it. And when I looked down, Rorie was in a tangle off to one side, bike wrapped around legs, green spikes of hair on the ground.

I pulled my bike to the side, clipped out and wrenched my tire pump free of the frame. I ran to Rorie's side. There were a few scratches, but nothing major I could see—the padding in Rorie's kit had done its job, and Rorie had caught the fall with gloved hands.

"You alright? Can you get up? We need to go. Now." The policebots were right over our heads, and their whining was waking up the local zombies. Dead heads and blank eyes turned toward us, noses raised in the air to catch a scent.

"You ride really well," Rorie said.

"Thanks, but—" I said, taking hold under Rorie's armpits.

"No, I mean it. Really powerful. I wanted you to know that."

I pulled up, hard, trying to lift Rorie. "Thanks, but enough of this. You can tell me when we're out of here." Out of the corner of my eye, I saw a few dozen shufflers heading our way. Fortunately, there didn't appear to be any fast-twitchers amongst them. Yet.

"Sorry," Rorie said, and jerked an arm back, punching my thigh. Burning fire spread from the impact. Rorie shrugged out of my arms, dropped a syringe, and remounted the bicycle. "The policebots will airlift you out after you get bitten. The drugs should keep you from feeling any pain as you change. I'm just telling this because you helped me, you know."

I was holding my thigh in both hands, as the fire spread down to my toes and up to my groin. "What? Why?" Cliche, but I really wanted to know. Curiosity to the point of death; another remnant from our monkey days.

"Because the power plants pay me. They always need new, strong zombies on the generator cranks. And you ride really well. Powerful."

With that, Rorie was gone, the zombies were close, and the policebots were hovering overhead.

I staggered to my bike, clipped back in, and started to pedal. My one leg was dead, unable to push or pull. I lurched about horribly, barely able to keep ahead of the zombies. The policebots stayed directly over me, but it was all I could do.

There was no way I could get back to the tunnel. No way back to the water, much less off the island. But there was one place I could go. Call it my monkey instincts again.

Which is why I ended up spending three days on the sea lion's rock in the middle of the Central Park Zoo, surrounded by water. And beyond that, zombies.

Good thing I packed well. Energy bars will get you through anything.

As to how I escaped the island? Well, Rorie was right. I ride really well. Really well.

ON EACH OTHER'S TEAM

T. M. Tomilson

Hallie had bought the bike in a moment of weakness. After she bought it, all she did was look at it. She'd had a lot of fears wrapped up in that bike. Those fears mostly had to do with getting hit by a car, or falling off into traffic. She had told herself that these fears were irrational, had promised herself she'd ride to school early on a clear morning.

But by then it had been fall and it rained every day. The bike sat in her living room collecting dust. It became a makeshift coat rack and eventually disappeared beneath layers of cloth. Winter began with a light snow, and then early spring brought the zombie apocalypse. As excuses went, Hallie thought the zombie apocalypse was a good one.

But it had also meant she needed to get around more than ever. And get away.

She'd thrown out some of the stuff she'd bought with the road bike. The reflective gear. The fancy pedals with their matching shoes that clipped on. She'd kept the distance tracker, the magnetic hand pump, and the repair kit. While everyone else had been running for weapons and food stores, she'd kept to the repair and hobby stores. She'd picked up a better helmet, spare tubes and tires, and a comfortable backpack. With her cycling shorts and black windbreaker, she looked like the pro she'd never been.

No, that was wrong. She looked like the pro she was becoming.

As Hallie rode, she wrote a guide in her mind. It distracted her from the burn in her legs. She'd thought of a lot of different titles over her hours of cycling. She was particularly enamored with "On Each Other's Team: Cycling in the Post-Apocalyptic World."

Cycling burns a lot of calories. Keep this in mind. Before the zombies, many of us could afford to burn these calories just for kicks or for weight loss. But now we need to conserve our energy and be careful with our fuel. Be mindful that you're not pushing yourself past your limits. Take what is offered and offer what you can. We're all on each other's team now.

And whatever you do, keep these five rules in mind:

1. *Keep your repair kit stocked.*
2. *Never get caught out at night.*
3. *Check your gear at every stop.*
4. *Be mindful of fuel and distance.*
5. *Be prepared to run.*

Hallie glanced at her distance tracker—36 miles down today. Lynne's Town was just around the corner.

The pavement was cracked on this route but not as bad as in some other places. The trees hadn't yet started to reclaim the land. She slowed and then balanced on her bike as the guards opened Lynne's Town's repurposed metal gate.

"Hey, Surveyor. Got any letters?" One of the guards asked. She was kitted out in body armor and was resting a hunting rifle against her left shoulder. Atop all this was a big smile and a red and white cap with a fuzzy ball on the top.

"No. I've got a dictate for the mayor, though," Hallie replied. "And some news about the roads between here and Beale."

The guards exchanged glances. "You know the way then, Surveyor," red-and-white-cap said. "You spending the night here?"

Hallie glanced at the afternoon sun. "Yeah. Don't want to risk it."

"See you at the gathering, then."

Hallie nodded in agreement and rode her bike careful and slow down the path into the town square, then off to the right. The familiar grey-and-white Surveyor tent came into view, with its surrounding fence of broken bicycle wheels, rusting in the open air.

She parked her bike and went inside, dropping her backpack by the door. She'd rest a bit before the gathering, where she would have to recite all of her messages.

After removing her shoes and helmet, Hallie got as comfortable as she could on a cot. She dreamed of a light snow on decaying leaves and the sound of her university's bells until she was woken by a cough.

A woman was standing in the doorway of the tent. She wore a black headband, the symbol of a Runner heralding bad news. She'd go from tent to tent, home to home, alerting the town. "Zombies approaching from the west, Surveyor. You'll want to get to the east entrance."

They regarded each other for a moment. Hallie was exhausted. Her muscles were aching. She didn't want to get back on the bike, especially not with night approaching.

But the Runner's gaze was dark. "It's a horde. We've got firepower, but our fortifications won't hold up. Not since the last time." She shook her head. "We just finished rebuilding that section of wall last week."

"It's only 15 miles to the next town," Hallie said. "The road is good. Shadeville cleared the fallen trees."

The Runner nodded, looking grim, and pulled a parcel from the bag she carried. "Bread and honey." She tossed it on the cot next to Hallie and watched Hallie begin to put her shoes back on.

"Good luck. Make sure Shadeville is prepared."

"I'll see you there." But the Runner was already gone.

Hallie gathered her things. Then she was off, cycling against the flow of Lynne's Town. The women all had guns and supplies and were grim faced and determined, running toward the storm and nodding as they past her.

Hallie pedaled faster, down the hill between huts and around a small garden. A Runner opened the gate for her and waved her out into the open road in the falling dusk.

She could hear gunshots, not so distant, and then distant, and then swallowed by the wind. She kept pedaling and reset her distance tracker with one hand. Just 15 miles to go.

She rode steadily until her bike began dancing on the concrete. Cursing, Hallie slowed down. Her front tire was flat. She hadn't had time to check her gear. Foolish. She should have done that first. She flipped the bike over to inspect the tire and then glanced back in the direction she had come. The zombies were there, but so were strong walls and a lot of tough women with guns.

Safety, she thought, then shook her head. The next town had to be notified, so they could help Lynne's Town and to prepare their own defenses.

Hallie hunkered down and focused on checking for whatever had caused the flat, ignoring the swell of panic that a zombie would come out of the ditch or from behind her.

"Rule six," she said, keeping her breathing quiet and steady as she began to inflate the replacement tube. "It's okay to be afraid, but don't abandon your team, or your objective, or your purpose. Follow through. We've only got each other."

THE LONG WAR

Bob Simms

Angie turned in a slow circle. To the east and west the A2 stretched to the horizons, clogged with rusting vehicles. To the north, the ground dropped down in a steep embankment. It was the south that bothered her. Thick woods were beginning to encroach onto the road's shoulder.

"Do you remember films?" said Lisa.

"What?" Angie turned back to her companion. Lisa screwed up her face as she levered the tyre back onto the rim.

"You know. Movies."

"Of course."

"So in the movies, you just had to shoot a zombie in the head, right? Bang, and it was over. Why can't real life be like that?"

Angie turned back to the woods. Something rustled in the leaves. A bird?

"You ever have an intellectual conversation with one?"

"Ha! I guess not."

Angie shrugged. "No need for brains, then. No need for any central nervous system. All they need to do is breed, and no one ever needed brains for that." There was definitely something there in the long grass, by the hawthorn. "You done yet?"

"Nearly. Just need to pump it up and hope the patch holds." Lisa mounted the wheel onto her upended bike and gave it an experimental spin.

"Okay." Angie stepped over the central barrier and edged slowly towards the trees.

"What is it?" called Lisa. Angie ignored her. The hawthorn suddenly thrashed, causing her heart to jump into her throat.

"Angie? What is it?"

Angie stopped where the hard shoulder began and stared into the shadows. There was something there on the ground, something big. It jerked and she caught a glimpse of a limb. She turned and strode back to the bikes. Lisa stood there, pump in hand, searching her face.

"Zombie," confirmed Angie. She opened the lid of the bike trailer and rummaged through the containers of petrol they'd scavenged.

"It's not a dog, is it? I hate it when it's a dog. I had a dog, you know, Before."

Before. It always had a capital, even in speech. No one needed to ask before what.

Angie pulled a gallon Jerry can from the trailer. "No, it's not a dog." She shook it. Half full. She replaced it and hauled out a full one. Lisa caught the significance and her hand flew to her mouth.

"Oh God, really? Out here? What were they doing?"

Angie shrugged. "Masks and gloves," she said, pulling on her own. She unscrewed the top of the pressure sprayer and carefully filled it with the precious fuel, then pumped the handle until the pressure was right.

Lisa was masked already when Angie hoisted herself into the straps. She hefted a pickaxe in her gloved hands.

"Ready?" she said.

Angie shook her head. "Never am, not for this. Let's get it over with. And I don't care if it is a dog, anything comes out of that wood you smash its head in, right?"

"Right."

"And if it's... if it's not a dog, you do the same."

Lisa nodded, her eyes wide above the mask.

They made their way over the central barrier and across the cracked tarmac to the shoulder. The verge beyond sloped up to the wood. Under the trees a wooden fence peeked out here and there from a mess of brambles and bindweed. Lisa stopped three feet shy of the body and stared. Angie stepped up beside her.

“You need to go further on,” she said gently. “Between me and the woods. Lisa?”

“Yeah.” Lisa tore her gaze away. “Yeah, right. Further on. You think there’s more?”

“More like that? No. It’s days old. If there are any, they’ll not be in any state to bother us.” It was easier, calling them ‘it’. It was just meat, days old and rotting. It didn’t have a name. It had never laughed or had friends or...

Angie shook her head and forced herself to concentrate. It had been male, judging by the clothes, and mature, judging by its size. The flesh was purple-black. It lay face down where it had fallen. Bite marks on its leg indicated scavenging.

"Eyes and ears, Lisa. Something's had a bite of it." She glanced up. Lisa stood between her and the woods, but she was looking back, staring at the corpse. "For Christ's sake, Lisa, get your head on. Eyes front. Cover me."

"Right." Lisa turned back to the wood, shifting her weight nervously from foot to foot.

Angie held up the long nozzle and pressed the trigger, watching the spray of fuel arc through the air and cover the body. Suddenly it convulsed, limbs flying. Its head twisted and she saw the nightmare of a face contort. Lisa swore.

"Can't we kill it first?" she asked.

"It's dead already. Look at it. It's been dead for days. Weeks, probably. You know how it works. The virus causes random electrical spasms. Movement attracts predators. That's all it is. It's the virus trying to reproduce." Angie gave a vicious kick at the leaf mould, sending a wave of leaf matter and dirt over its head, hiding the obscene mockery of a face. "And if you don't want to end up the same way, keep your bloody eyes on the wood. A fox or something has been at it."

She made sure Lisa was watching the woods before she resumed spraying the corpse.

"It's never going to end, is it?" said Lisa. Angie glanced up. At least Lisa was still facing the wood.

"Yeah, it will, eventually. Not tomorrow, and not completely, but it'll get better. We've just got to keep fighting it. Eventually it'll burn itself out. It has to. It'll run out of hosts, reproduction will slow, and we'll develop a resistance. In the end it'll be like the Black Death, consigned to remote pockets, and then, eventually, it'll be just history."

"Not in our lifetime."

The sprayer sputtered and spat the last of the petrol onto the body. Angie pulled out the matches. "Maybe not, but that's not the point. We keep fighting it now, so it ends in somebody's lifetime."

She struck the match and started the fire.

THE BREEDERS

Emily June Street

My cotton underwear felt oddly sticky between my thighs. I rose and pulled down my pajama shorts. Shock, horror, and a tiny drop of wonder bubbled in my stomach. *What the hell?* A big splotch marred my underwear. It was definitely blood, still damp.

"Holy crap." My whole body trembled as I considered the ramifications of this blood.

I pulled out fresh underwear and the cotton undershirt I wore beneath my work jumpsuit, tearing the tee into shreds to soak up the blood. I burned the stained panties in the bathroom sink.

"It's Maddy Morgan," I said into my comm-box. "I woke up this morning feeling off. Some kind of stomach bug. I'm taking a sick day."

I tried to recall what women did about the blood before the Event, but I had only been a few years old. I had always assumed I would be like the vast majority of women who came of age after the Event—so messed up hormonally that I'd never menstruate or be fertile. From what I could recall of my mom, she must have worked right through her cycle. I shivered. Work was not an option. Any engineered nose would smell my blood a block away.

I lay on my bed, kneading my sore belly. I felt jittery and more than a little scared. No one talked much about the Event—a worldwide plague, alien attack, or massive experiment gone wrong, depending on whom you asked. We'd all simply accommodated ourselves to its effects, the main one being human reproductive failure.

About seven years before, Sector scientists had perfected "a viable reproductive alternative." Basically, it amounted to reanimating preserved dead bodies—rich people who had been cryofrozen using experimental technologies back in the twentieth and twenty-first centuries. They had wanted to live forever and were now having their moment. Their century-old corpses were being defrosted and reanimated. Unfortunately, only the male gametes proved viable.

This left women like me—the one percent who produced eggs and menstruated against all odds—to provide the other half of the equation. "For the good of the species," as the slogan went.

Unless I wanted to become Breeder Camp's latest poster child, I'd need to lay low for at least five days. Could a sense-enhanced agent detect my fertility aside from smelling my blood? Were there other associated odors? I didn't know.

First thing, I needed to get more tee shirts to make more pads. I had to risk one outing. I grabbed Blue, my bike, a triumph of parts scavenged from junkyards far and wide, and pedaled to the local supply shop, avoiding official jumpsuits.

I felt safe enough buying a stack of new tee shirts from Harold's supply shop. He wasn't a bounty hunter. I tossed the package in Blue's basket and headed home.

Before I'd gotten even a hundred yards up the block, a shout rang behind me. "You! You there, on the blue bike!"

I braked and stepped a foot down to glance over my shoulder. "Can I help you?"

A tall woman with a heavy bun of hair approached. Damn—she wore a white jumpsuit.

I mounted Blue and started to pedal away.

"Hey!" the woman cried. "Stop! I've got a stungun trained on your back. Stop now!"

I didn't stop. The shot hit me like a boulder. I froze mid-pedal and toppled. Blue crashed on top of me. The woman approached, leaned over, and *sniffed* me, like a dog meeting a rival. "I knew I smelled blood."

I tried to move, but the stungun had done its job. The woman handcuffed me and then injected me with stun antidote. “On your feet, kid. You’re coming with me.”

With her stungun trained on my back, I didn’t have a choice. My shirts, fallen from Blue’s basket, lay strewn over the street like spilled milk. “What about my bike?”

“Leave it. You won’t need it where you’re going.” The woman herded me into a white minivan parked near Harold’s shop. She opened the sliding door, pulled out a comm-box, and typed furiously with only one hand.

“In you go.”

• • •

The van drove beyond the city, the food-farm camp, and the dry lake, and passed through a final security checkpoint. We pulled up at a concrete compound, the kind of square cinder block construction that was the hallmark of post-Event architecture, as if we had to reflect the starkness of our world in our buildings.

Bunhead the bounty-hunter let me out of the van. A sign hung above the entry into the compound. The pink thing on it was meant to be a uterus.

She strode up the steps beneath the sign. We passed through a hall with no decoration and entered a conference room filled by a large table and six chairs.

"Have a seat," Bunhead directed.

Another white-jumpsuited woman arrived bearing a medical tray loaded with paper and implements. "I'm Doctor Carter," she said, exchanging a glance with Bunhead, who gave an ominous nod.

Dr. Carter asked for my ID. I handed it over reluctantly.

"Madyson Morgan," she read, pinching her long nose with her fingers. "Age: twenty years." She flipped through more papers before cocking an eyebrow. "We'll run a basic test."

"My nose is never wrong," Bunhead said. "She's menstruating."

"Is this your first cycle?" Dr. Carter asked me in a cold, clinical tone.

"W—what?" I stammered.

"Don't bother lying," Bunhead snapped.

Carter took a syringe from the tray, jabbed it into my arm, and siphoned my blood with businesslike aplomb. "I'll test this and be right back."

Bunhead folded her arms and glared at me. Carter returned. "Congratulations, Ms. Morgan, you're fertile. Follow me, please."

I didn't want to go with her, and as I followed with leaden feet, I felt weirdly despondent about Blue, abandoned. Would someone else find her and make use of her?

The doctor led me up a set of stairs and down a lifeless hall. "This will be your dorm room," she announced as she opened a door.

The room contained two twin beds, a table, and a lamp.

"You'll be under observation. In a week, if all goes well, we'll make our first insemination attempt. Twelve! Get out of the closet!"

I blinked. A large figure emerged from the closet, half-dressed in a plain jumpsuit not yet buttoned. She stood six feet tall, muscled across the chest like a bodybuilder. The babies who had been in utero during the Event had come out a little different—some with female parts but an almost male physique, some with male parts but feminine features. Many of these young people had fled to Libber's Camps out west where they wouldn't end up at the mercy of Sector scientists who wanted to study them for clues to the Event mystery. Rumor said there were even people in the Libber's camps with viable sperm, and that some people were able to reproduce the old fashioned way out there.

"Twelve will guide you through your daily schedule." Carter gave a curt nod and stepped from the room.

"Is this—uh—normal?" I wondered.

Twelve snorted. "What the hell is normal?"

"I mean, is this how it's usually done? When a new recruit arrives?"

"There haven't been that many."

"Twelve can't be your real name."

"I'm Twelve because I was the twelfth recruit. And guess what? You're Thirteen."

"They're breeding you?"

"I've got the right parts, I had a period, and I got caught. Anyone who bleeds breeds. Doesn't matter how you feel about it."

"So umm—how do they do it?"

"Do what?" Twelve flopped onto the nearest bed, her legs so long her feet hung off the edge.

"The breeding. I mean, do we have to—uh—mate—with a defrosted corpse?" The very idea of having to touch—much less copulate with—a zombie sent shivers down my spine.

"You've got quite the imagination," Twelve said. "Don't worry; this isn't like some Margaret Atwood novel from the twentieth century. They do it all artificially. You just lie there while they squirt the stuff up your cunt. Like how they used to do it with horses or endangered species. It's no worse than a pelvic exam."

I sat on the edge of the other bed. "I don't want to breed. And I don't want a pelvic exam, either."

"They don't give a damn what you want. It's all about what they want. And what they want is babies. Sexually-reproduced babies, not clones, not resurrected zombies. They want the benefits of sexual reproduction—stronger immune systems, genetic variety, all that shit from eighth-grade science."

Twelve rolled onto her side and propped her head on her arm. "Just keep your head down and follow the rules. Eat what they tell you to eat, do what they tell you to do." Her eyes—one blue, one green—flashed. "Don't take the yellow pills; those ones mess with your head. The pink ones jack with your hormones. I spit them both out, but it's the yellow ones that'll make you vegetative." She rolled to a seat and placed both feet on the linoleum, leaning across the gap between our beds. "I've got a plan."

"What?"

"A plan. To get out."

"To escape?"

"Hell yes. But we've gotta lay low for a week or two. I'm still researching. I'll need your help when the time comes, that's why I'm telling you. Just keep your mouth shut, follow the schedule, and don't take the yellow pills."

• • •

Our daily schedule started with "a healthy, well-rounded breakfast." If we didn't finish our food, we had to drink a disgusting shake to make up the difference in calories—each woman in the Breeder Camp was required to consume 2,000 calories per day until she conceived, and more after.

In addition to being nearly force-fed—Five once refused to eat and they did stick a feeding tube down her throat. We had to drink fluids after every meal—a full 32 ounces of water adulterated with minerals and electrolytes. It made me nearly vomit every time.

Our recreation hour was the only time we had to ourselves. The rest of the day, camp workers—

"techs"—observed us. But during rec hour the techs took their lunch. We were expected to walk laps around a courtyard, or we could use the stationary bikes on the lowest setting.

On my seventh day in the Breeder Camp, Twelve and I scrambled onto the exercise bikes during rec hour. Twelve had been inseminated the day before, leaving her tetchy and annoyed. She scowled as she pedaled.

"Do you see that?" she demanded out of the blue. I followed her pointing finger to a latch on the front stem of the stationary bike. "What about it?" I was feeling gloomy myself. Carter had scheduled me to be inseminated the following morning. I didn't like the idea of being impregnated by a cold metal tube any more than I liked the notion of carrying a reanimated corpse's DNA.

"The bike detaches," Twelve muttered.

"Huh?" I peered closer. "It's a functioning bike, not just an exercise bike?"

“Back in the 21st there was this big push to improve public health. Someone had this idea that people should bike at their workstations and then they could detach the bike to ride around on their lunch break or commute home.” Twelve gestured at the bike beneath her. “The WerkBike was born.”

I much preferred to ride a real bike, even in boring laps, to a stationary one. “How do you detach it?” Twelve shook her head. “Can’t. The head tech has the key.”

“Damn.”

Twelve leaned precariously on her WerkBike so she could speak near my ear. “Getting the key is part one of my plan.”

“You mean to—you mean to escape *by bike*?”

Twelve broke into a grin. “Think how much farther you can travel in a day by bike rather than on foot.”

“You’ll never get the key.”

“Wait and see.” Twelve pedaled faster, jutting her chin at the back of the courtyard. “That sliding gate opens right to the outdoors. Flat, dry, empty land. Freedom.”

The WerkBikes tracked our energy usage and reported it to the techs—we weren’t allowed to burn more than 150 calories during our exercise hour. Twelve pedaled even harder, shaking her WerkBike in its stand. The other women in the rec yard, Five, Seven, and Nine, kept a close eye on Twelve as they walked their laps together.

“Careful. You’ll bring a tech out into the courtyard,” I said as Twelve pedaled hard. By silent consensus, we all avoided bringing the techs to our only private place.

Twelve grinned. “That’s the idea. When you have a chance, take it.”

Before I could ask what she meant, the door to the compound flew open and the head tech bustled over, scowling. His badge hung around his neck and a set of keys jangled at his hip.

He slammed a palm across Twelve's console to cut the bike's power. Not that it made any difference; Twelve kept pedaling like a maniac, standing up as though she raced some imaginary opponent.

"What's wrong with you?" the tech demanded. "You've just had your treatment. It's important to keep your body calm."

Twelve ignored him. He rifled in his pockets and withdrew a capped syringe. I slid down from my Werkbike.

The tech reached for Twelve's arm, but she thrust a punch, catching him on the temple. He collapsed, clutching his head.

I unhooked his carabiner of keys.

Twelve caught my eye and nodded. The other women had gathered to watch the ruckus. Seven stood just behind me, hands folded on her swelling belly.

"Get the handset," she muttered. "Otherwise he'll call in the others."

I snatched the tech's comm-box and shoved it into my jumpsuit. Meanwhile, Twelve had pinned the tech while Five shucked off her jumpsuit and tore it into long strips to tie and gag the man.

Once the tech was immobilized, I handed Twelve the keys. She pulled one off the carabiner and tossed it to Seven, who hurried to the sliding gate. Twelve leaned over her WerkBike, unlocked it from its console, and then moved down the line of bikes, doing the same for each. Five and Nine rolled open the gate, exposing the barren landscape beyond the Breeder compound.

I caught the handlebars of the bike Twelve pushed at me. Twelve and Seven led us through the gate,

pedaling madly. The WerkBikes had thick tires that could cope with the bumpy ground.
"We stay off the roads," Twelve commanded. "They'll search there first."

We fell into a formation, Twelve leading the way.

"If we don't use the road, how will we know where we're going?" Five called. "Isn't it all Event wasteland around here?"

"I know where I'm going," Twelve said. "I used to ride single-track out here when I was kid. They've only got cars at the Breeder's camp. They won't be able to follow where we're going."

Nine said, "They'll send sense-enhanced agents and bounty hunters to track us. Eventually they'll call in their resources—helicopters, ATVs, all that."

I silently agreed with her concern.

Twelve stood up and pedaled harder. "Pick up the pace. We need to get lost quickly." She cut onto a narrow path, just barely visible, that ran across the parched earth. The track dove downhill into a gully. Despite the treacherous descent, I understood Twelve's object: to hide us from view of the camp. We rode along a dry creek bed at the bottom of the gully, heading due west as the sun slipped below the horizon.

Finally Twelve answered Nine's question. "There's a place out west, a Libbers' Camp—people who left the Sectors and dropped out. They farm their own food and get by on their own, self-subsisting. If we can get there ahead of the search parties, the Libbers will let us in and give us asylum."

More than once, after a long, soul-numbing day of harassment at work, I'd fantasized about riding off into the sunset on Blue to try to find a Libbers' Camp.

"How far is it?" Seven murmured. She was the only one of us noticeably pregnant.

"A rough 45 miles," Twelve replied. "But we're all in perfect health—the Breeders made sure of that. It'll be tough, but if we just keep pedaling, we'll make it. Whatever you do, don't give up. We've got to keep moving."

I pedaled as fast as I could, wishing I had Blue in all her custom glory instead of the WerkBike. But any bike was better than no bike, and as we rode into freedom, I tried to imagine life in a Libber's camp. Were there Libber men who could reproduce, as the rumors said? The thought of having a baby wasn't so bad if I got to choose when, where, and with whom it happened. Sudden excitement about my body's newfound ability coursed through my veins. My menstrual blood was a blessing now that I was free.

I might like being a mother.

The Biking Dead

YOU TWO SURE YOU DON'T WANNA COME?
SOUNDS LIKE WORK.
I JUST PUT THE COOKIES IN.
SIGH FINE. I GUESS I'LL BE THE ONLY ONE WHO'S PREPARED WHEN OUR LIVES BECOME A ZOMBIE MOVIE...
PFFT.
DUDE... YOU'D TOTALLY BE THE FIRST TO GO DOWN.

ZOMBIE BIKE RIDE

JOLENE?
WHY'S THE PORCH LIGHT OFF?
ERICA?
...THIS ISN'T FUNNY, YOU GUYS...

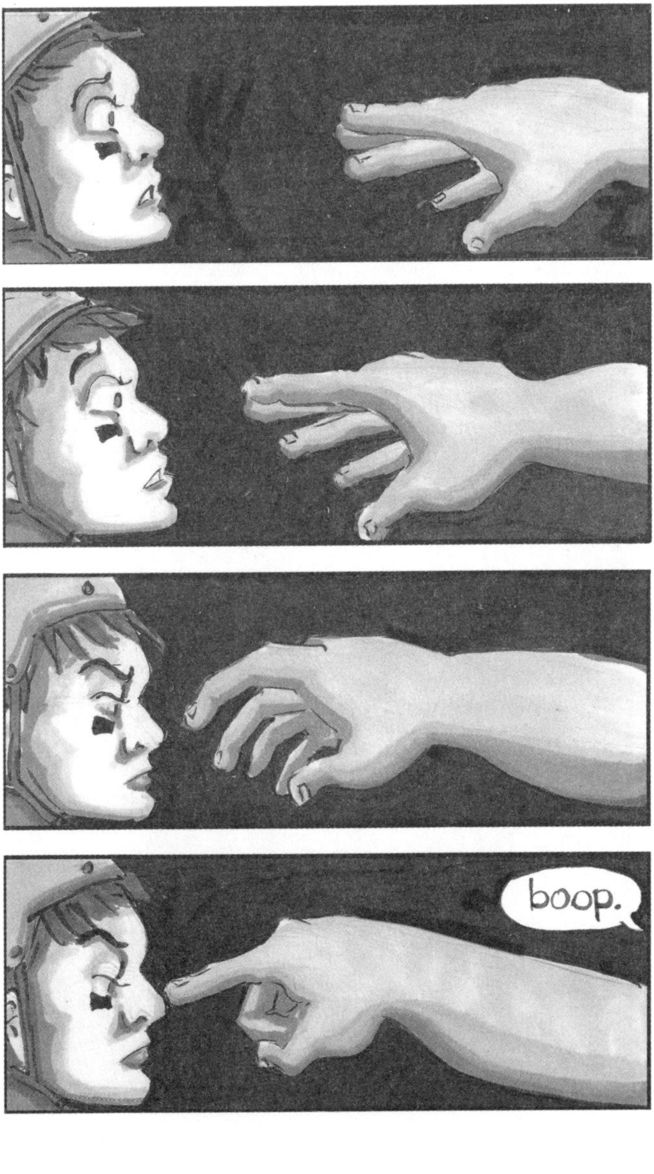
boop.

ERICA!
OH GOD... YOUR FACE...
COME ON, ZOMBIE HUNTER.
UGH... THERE HAD BETTER BE COOKIES LEFT...
(DID YOU STEAL MY EYELINER?)
(...WE MIGHT HAVE.)
The End

PEDALING SQUARE

David J. Fielding

She kept pedaling.

She had lost her left shoe on the outskirts of Tempe. At least she thought it was Tempe.

She couldn't remember exactly.

Her brain was fried. She couldn't think straight. Her mind stuttered. Her thoughts were... fragmented, yes, that was the word. Wasn't it? She couldn't be sure. One thought flipped to another, rapid-fire, manic, ADD; some connected, others not.

She kept pedaling.

She had lost her left shoe on the outskirts of Tempe. It could've been Mesa, or Glendale, or Scottsdale, hell, any one of those suburbs surrounding Phoenix. It was hard to remember. But, she thought, it has to have been outside of Tempe. She had been heading north and then east, trying to stay ahead of it. The only clear thing she remembered about those terror-filled hours were jump-cut scenes of blood, horror, running, and screaming.

And that she'd lost her shoe.

She'd liked that shoe. It was comfortable.

She missed that shoe.

She kept pedaling.

At least she had gotten out alive.

The only other thing she could recall was the constant pall of dread over the uncounted days she had been on the run. There wasn't anything else.

No bills, no job, no obligations or tasks to be done. No clients to meet, no friends to see, no husband at the end of the day. In an instant all of that was gone. They were all gone. She was alone.

All she knew was desert, heat, dust, and thirst.

Everything else blurred into a haze of sleeplessness, gnawing hunger, and fatigue.

The sun rose, the sun set, a blazing hot, unfeeling deity. The bright moon sailed east to west silently across the star-pocked sky, a cold and uncaring lover. Both shone down impassively on a stark, blasted, empty landscape.

She kept pedaling.

Bone-weary with exhaustion, she no longer felt the metal teeth of the pedal cutting into her raw, bloody foot. All she could hear was the steady creak of the Huffy's wheels and chain as she crept along at a snail's pace, heading east.

It seemed she was the only living thing on this stretch of 66.

She kept pedaling.

Her pace was bad, she knew that. Couldn't be helped. Wasn't a damn racing bike anyway.

Still, she knew she could do better. She was pedaling square, not rhythmically, as she'd learned so many years ago on the pace line, and that was what was tiring her out. And now her fingers were getting stiff.

The sky was hot and a dusky, burnt orange behind her. Every now and then she would risk a look back. Not too often, though, because the highway was littered with things that could send her into a tumble. She'd learned that the hard way. Luckily she'd had enough distance on them and she was able to get back up and going before they gained too much ground.

The color of the sky told her it was going to get dark soon.

There was one more day gone.

Her shoulder ached, the one she'd fallen on. Scraped it bad, she guessed. It felt like she'd fallen on a board full of nails. The street she'd been running had been crowded and littered with debris, so it was possible. She remembered that others had fallen too. That was just after she had lost the shoe, she thought, but she couldn't really remember.

She had checked her shoulder right away and then again much later, and each time and her hand came away thick with red. She didn't understand how the scrape could be so bad. The pain of it had been flaring again this last hour and the ache was spreading down her side.

She kept pedaling.

Her tongue felt fat. There wasn't any spit to moisten it. Could you choke on your own tongue? She remembered reading that somewhere. She put her foot down, the one that still had a shoe, and tapped it along the road, slowly jerking to a stop.

Her vision blurred, like her thoughts. She fumbled around for the fanny pack, and then remembered the water bottle had been tossed out... when? A day ago? Two?

She needed water.

That meant she had to look in cars again. She hated looking in cars. The highway was littered with them, abandoned during the panic. Sometimes there would be one of the things trapped in there, clawing pathetically at the windows, too mindless to open the door.

She gazed wearily at the double lines of vehicles leading away from her, then back over her shoulder at the frozen traffic leading all the way back to the city. A few lights were still on back there. The things were back there, too.

She should put more distance between her and them.

She kept pedaling.

The sun was gone now, and dark descending. She stopped the bike, stumbled to the nearest car. There was still light enough to see by. Nothing inside. She moved to the next, and the next, and the next. The fifth one had a little boy in it, maybe seven years old. Skin the color of wax paper, eyes rolled back, mouth opening and closing, teeth bared; feral.

She moved on. The next car had a cooler in the back seat. The doors were locked, but she picked up a rock off the side of the road and after ten or twelve tries busted the window in. The water was warm, bath water temperature. But it was wet. Most of it spilled down the front of her, but she got some down.

She went back, picked up the bike and straddled it. Her shoulder creaked with agony and it was creeping up her neck now. Infected? Maybe. She'd worry about that tomorrow. She had to keep moving.

She kept pedaling.

The night air grew chill, and the further out she got from the city, the less she had to weave in and out between the cars. She just kept moving by instinct. Pumping her legs had become second nature. Her mind begged for sleep, but she just kept seeing their open mouths, black bile, gnashing blood-stained teeth. If she fell asleep, they'd catch her.

Her mind buzzed. It wasn't a headache. Not this time, just a steady, whirring buzz. That scrape on her shoulder, caused by the fall, she knew that. Not from the man who grabbed her as she ran, no. He hadn't bitten her, hadn't got that close. No, she was sure of that. She'd gotten away from him.

Then she'd lost her shoe.

She'd liked that shoe.

All those fragmented thoughts and images lost color and shape. Her mouth began to work up and down unconsciously. Her eyes glazed over. The only thing she saw was the skin of her arms, pale and yellowish, and her claw-like hands clamped on the handlebars.

Her legs were moving up and down, simply on impulse.

Her last thought ... just keep going.

Keep going. Keep going...

It kept pedaling.

INTERCHANGE

Ellie Poley

Interstate 74 stretched, empty, as far as Sofia could see. Autumn leaves crunched under her tires as she pedaled. She shared the road only with the crows, which always cawed at her when she passed: *Get off the road! Highways are for birds, not bikes!*

Her longtail was loaded down with veggies and milk she had picked up for her housing block's community supper. Something about the crisp air on her skin made her feel alive and powerful, and pedaling had become effortless. When she saw the faded sign for exit 48, she shifted up and pedaled hard. Flying down the cloverleaf off-ramp was always the best part of the ride—the faster, the better.

Just as she was rounding the middle of the ramp, she saw a human-like figure stumbling across the lane.

"Aaaaah!" Sofia braked and swerved. She could hardly see the thing's face as she passed it, but she knew she needed to get the hell away, fast. She hadn't seen a zombie since she was eight, but the same primal terror rose up in her gut like it had never left. *Oh god, oh god. I thought they were extinct.*

She pedaled furiously down the last half of the ramp. As the curve leveled out, she looked behind her to see how much space remained between herself and the undead; whether she stood a chance of escape...

But it wasn't chasing her. It was standing right where Sofia had passed it.

"Hey!" it shouted.

Sofia stopped and turned around. She took a deep breath. This wasn't a zombie—but why would a person be walking around on the old interstate?

As Sofia approached the person, she tried to take them in. Youngish, like her... but dressed too neatly to belong here. They were clearly distressed, but they didn't look dangerous.

"Are you okay?" Sofia asked.

The person just stared at Sofia and her bike; they looked dazed.

"Okay. Well I'm Sofia; I use *she* and *her* as pronouns. What about you?"

"Um, Arri. *She* and *her*."

"Hi, Arri. I don't mean to be rude, but what are you doing here? You okay?"

Arri looked away.

"All right, you don't have to tell me..." Sofia said.

"What is this thing?" Arri asked.

"It's a called a 'bicycle.' It's a type of vehicle that you power by pedaling with your legs."

"Oh, like a small... what were they called..."

"...car?"

"Yeah!"

"Nah, they had electric engines; no pedaling."

"I see..." Arri started. "So why would you use a bicycle?"

Sofia paused. "Well, I started biking when I was a kid, before the zombie eradication. This was how my family escaped—"

"Oh, before they invented teleport evasion?"

"Well, ah, no. We couldn't 'port."

"Huh?"

"My family immigrated here, so we can't get chipped."

Arri looked uncomfortable. "You're not chipped?"

"Shit. Maybe I should go. Nice meeting you, Arri." Sofia grabbed her handlebars.

"No! Don't. I won't report you. I just didn't know that there were... you know, people like you."

"People like me."

"Sorry! I mean... Sorry. Please stay."

"Okay. You're not going to turn me in to the Teleporter Authority. That's real nice. And I can tell you're not trying to be as mean as you sound right now. But I really have to get back home with this food, or my neighbors aren't going to eat dinner tonight. So do you want to cut to the point and tell me what you're doing here?"

"I got into a teleporting accident. I don't know what happened. I was heading to Chicago—"

"We're about 150 miles from there," Sofia interrupted.

"Oh."

"Isn't that why you have a beacon mode? Press a button and someone will come find you?" Sofia asked.

"It will notify my parents. They're not supposed to know I'm here—they think I'm getting dinner with an aunt in Amsterdam right now."

"I see..."

Silence.

"You'd rather starve out here than have your parents find you?"

"Well... Maybe you can help me?"

"How?"

"I don't know; I was hoping you had an idea." Arri smiled a little, for the first time since Sofia had met her.

Arri's smile dissolved the last of Sofia's physical defenses. Suddenly she felt warm; she felt like something inside her, around her hips, was tugging softly towards Arri.

"Okay." Sofia smiled back. "I think I have something."

"Yeah?"

"Well, there's a teleport in the town... I could give you a ride there. I'm heading home anyway. "

"A ride?"

"On the bike. Bicycle."

"Is it dangerous?" Arri asked.

"Only when there are stranded 'porters wandering like zombies in the middle of the road," Sofia smirked.

"Sorry."

"Listen, riding a bike is probably the most fun you'll have all year. Trust me. We'll get you out of here."

Sofia straddled the bike and showed Arri the stoker bars.

"Hop on."

The extra weight sent them flying fast down the incline of the ramp, even as it leveled out onto Main Street.

Sofia figured Arri had probably never traveled any speed other than walking pace or the speed of light. "You all right?" she yelled back to Arri.

"Yeah!"

Sofia turned back to look at her. Arri looked less like the composed, well-dressed out-of-towner Sofia had just been talking to. The clip had fallen out of her hair, and her careful beauty gave way to something more joyful and radiant. They shared a smile.

It was a strange, lovely sensation for Sofia to have another person, an almost-friend, on the bike with her. She usually spent at least half her day on the bike; she would have no freedom, no independence, and no work without it. Days on the bike were usually quiet and peaceful, but she was almost always alone.

“What’s that?” Arri asked, pointing to a crumbling building they were approaching.

“Oh, that’s the Mickey Dee’s. It was a cheap restaurant in the old time. Nowadays the kids just use the play area. I go in there now and then to make sure the slides are still holdin’ together.”

“So you work here?”

"Yeah, kind of."

They pedaled on, into the old downtown, past the apartment buildings beyond there.

"Sofia, where is everyone? What is this place?"

"This town is a sort of 'porter-slum, that's what they call them," Sofia said. "Most of the folks around here teleport to work, you know, cleaning buildings or serving food in Tokyo or Barcelona."

"But not you."

"No. I stick around here, doing odd jobs and stuff for them while they're at work. I watch the little ones 'til they get their 'chips, repair their home-bots, you know... They trade me for a place to live or food, maybe a little money when things are good."

"Wow. I guess... I guess I didn't know people lived in places like this."

Sofia suppressed a sigh. As much as she wanted to badge this woman as privileged and clueless, she had to remind herself that it wasn't her fault; the global society was designed this way. After the zombie threat was gone, teleporting became a form of everyday transportation, but it was also a tool to keep class boundaries rigid and invisible. "Where are you from, Arri?"

"I live with my parents in San Francisco, and I work in Dubai."

"So, you never noticed that everyone who lives around you was, you know, doing pretty well? And the maids and nannies and janitors just kind of came and left? Where did you think those folks were 'porting from?"

"I... don't know. I guess I didn't think... I'm sorry."

"Don't apologize. I didn't mean to put you on the spot. Not too many people know how it really is," Sofia said.

They rode in silence for the last few minutes.

“Here we are,” Sofia said as they approached her neighborhood’s teleport. She parked the bike and held Arri’s arm while she swung her leg over the deck.

“It was nice meeting you, Arri,” Sofia said as she walked her towards the port. “I hope life treats you well.”

“Thank you,” Arri said softly, and pulled Sofia into a hug. “I wish you the same.”

Arri stepped back, and Sofia started towards her bike. Arri stared up at the teleport, and flipped open the touchpad embedded in her forearm.

“Whatcha doing?” Sofia asked.

“Taking down the port number.”

Sofia smiled. “I’ll see you again?”

"Yeah. Are you going to be around here this weekend?"

"Where else would I go?" Sofia laughed.

"Cool. Maybe you can show me how to ride your bike?"

DEADMONTON

Alexandrea Flynn

"*Nîtisânak.*" Janey called the meeting to order. Conversations gradually ceased as we turned our attention to the de facto leader of our cooperative. Janey had come up with the idea of using her language, Cree, as the identifier for our collective. A quick way to identify friendlies was by greeting them with '*nîtisân*' – my sibling. If they were part of our larger cooperative they would know the appropriate response. "*Nimis,*" we replied in near unison. Seated to Janey's left, on a repurposed gym bench in what had once been the fitness room of a luxury apartment building, I continued to add screw-spikes to the 26-inch tire I was working on.

Our collective was diverse; most of our members were First Nations, like Janey, or former street kids or homeless folks who already knew how to survive on nothing. Formerly middle-class folks like me, Mike, and Ric were rare in inner-city collectives. The groups we allied with in the larger cooperative were usually more homogeneous, brought together by shared culture or neighbourhood.

“Snow is already falling in Terwilligar,” Janey continued. The once-affluent area was the farthest south our linked cooperative reached, but we had broader contacts thanks to Ric’s old CB radio. “Ric heard from our radio contact in Muskwacis that the drop in temperature has already slowed down the latest wave of H8Cher’s moving up from Idaho.”

Muskwacis was a First Nations Reservation an hour south of the city; many reservations had survived the virus and the resulting panic by being both off the beaten path and unknown to most non-Aboriginals. Muskwacis, located too near a major highway, had taken heavy losses in the recent waves of both panicked refugees and the virus-driven undead that chased them.

“How did they get past Calgary?” someone called out.

“Fucking ZedH8Cher’s” and similar curses peppered the crowd. ZH81 was the official CDC code for the virus that had quickly spread from initial cases in the Carolinas, mutating its way west and reaching Portland and the Mexican border in just eight months. Four months after that, the first Canadian cases were reported in Winnipeg just in time for the spring thaw. The Panic saw hordes of Americans fleeing both north and south in the mistaken belief that somehow the virus couldn't cross the borders. But we do have one defense they don't: Edmonton sits on the 53rd parallel north of the Equator and is famous for its long winters; extreme cold is one of the best defenses against the ZH81 zombies.

"We haven't heard from Calgary since last month," Ric, Janey's ex-military boi-friend, called out. This quieted some; others kept on muttering to each other. "At this point we have to assume they're gone or fighting for their lives."

Back in the days before The Panic, the drive from Calgary to Edmonton typically took three and a half hours on a busy highway famous for its speed traps and winter pile-ups. It had long since turned into a wasteland of abandoned vehicles looted of valuables and surrounded by corpses—both human and H8Cher.

"It is our sixth winter," Janey continued once the grumbling had settled down. "The cold is our ally. We all know H8Cher's move slower in the snow." I stabbed another screw through the tire and thought of my wife Giselle; we had escaped Winnipeg before the first wave of panicked USian refugees stormed the border. She'd been killed by one of them for the 4 gallons of unfiltered river water she was hauling back from the river; I'd caught a bullet in my arm trying to rescue her. That had been our second summer in Edmonton, the third year of our marriage.

Following Giselle's death we had switched from pairs to squads of four at all times: three on mountain bikes armed with hand guns and bladed weapons and one Yuba rider armed with a rifle and carrying improvised Katana staffs. With six much-coveted Yuba bikes, which we had modified for even greater cargo capacity, we were the best armed and supplied collective in the area.

"Paula?" Janey broke through my grief-filled thoughts. "How are your preparations?"

I held up the tire I had been spiking. "All but two of our bikes are fully winterized. We'll be ready to go by morning," I said, looking from Janey to Mike; he and I were the only Jamaicans in our collective. He was my second in command and my closest friend. "Mike and I are almost finished with the patrol rota but we need a few more volunteers." Janey looked concerned.

"Two of our guys are about to give birth," Mike said with his most charming smile. There were many more smiles as all eyes turned towards Mariam and Juliana, the pregnant couple who would soon add to the small number of children in our collective. Mariam was a true Edmontonian - kicked out by her religious parents for being queer. Her partner, Juliana, was a Brazilian international student studying biochemistry when the government fell and ideas like nationality and borders became moot. They'd met in the collective.

"They'll be back on their bikes soon enough. Still," Mike scanned the crowd, "the more patrol riders we have, the better off we are."

Janey looked around the crowd, waiting for members to volunteer for the dangerous reconnaissance duty. "I can spare a few hours tomorrow morning," Janey stated. Three, then five, hands shot up to volunteer. Mike and I shared a look and I made a mental note of who would need white, winter camo in the morning.

Once the government fell into chaos and the gas ran out, the SUV-driving suburban crowd, who had managed to survive thanks to their mobility, turned on each other. The suburbs became warzones; only those smart enough to hide themselves or escape to the river valley lived. A small group of them, led by a librarian, had taken up residence in a former convent. They were our Terwilligar contacts, going by the handle 'Providence.' Some of them would be joining us on our mission in the morning.

"We'll take three Yubas in the morning, and as many outriders as we can spare. Dan is our best scout; he'll set out before dawn." Dan Cardinal was leaning against the boarded-up picture window, the pinkish light of dusk from the peephole made a bright mask around is eyes, he nodded just enough to acknowledge Janey's directions without moving his gaze. "Providence is sending two scouts on skis. They'll be there to meet Dan."

The room was remarkably quiet, considering there were close to 75 people crammed into the space. Janey stood up to end the meeting when someone near the back called out.

"Wait—which Yubas?" It sounded like Carly, one of our trappers; a significant skill in a city over-run with hares and coyotes. It was a risk to take three of our most valuable assets on the same mission. Regular bikes were fairly easy to repair and replace, but the long-tailed, cargo-bearing Yubas were too important for our survival. Carly had voiced what many in the room were likely thinking.

"Including the green," Janey said. She shoved her hands into her pockets as the collective voices cried out with anger or dismay. The green Yuba was our arsenal bike; its rear rack was covered in rip-stop nylon camo to disguise the fact that it carried our sole rocket launcher between two side-racks packed with automatic weapons, ammo, and our cache of grenades. Mike and I had spent two weeks kitting out that rack; we considered it our best work.

"Are we suddenly going on the offensive?" Liam asked above the din of similar questions. From the start we had a clear policy: Kill H8cher's whenever possible, harm other humans only in self-defense. It was one of the ideals that held our group together. We would not become like the myopic bastards who had caused the carnage we were living through.

"No, No!" Janey yelled, and the group quieted slightly. "Just in case it's needed. I'm not telling anyone to attack when we don't yet know what we're dealing with." People were nervous, but starting to move, standing up to go back to our duties. "Together!" she yelled out the traditional closing chant.

"We are stronger!" We called out as a group. As the last few non-patrol members headed out of the door, Mike called out in his jovial way.

"When you meet the H8cher on the road..."

"Kill the H8cher" the patrol members replied.

We left before the sun was up. An hour earlier, Dan had slipped into the swirling snow, swaddled in white from head to toe. His route would be more direct than ours since he was running in snow shoes. We would have to trust that he would post signals on the bike path telling us if the bridge was still a safe crossing.

Providence informed us that their watchtower had spotted a church squad migrating from Twin Brooks down the Whitemud ravine to take up residence on the old Fort Edmonton site. During the initial panic many chose to hunker down in their religious communities to pray away the ZH81 zombies. The few church groups that had actually prepped for disaster did okay for the first year, but there was more than one horror story. The surviving church squads were twitchy; this was well known. That this one had left their secure compound for a disused historical theme park suggested they were running for their lives.

We approached the Quesnell Bridge bike path from Laurier Drive 25 minutes after we left home. The world was still a swirl of fat snowflakes. As we approached the bridge, I saw the pale green scrap of flagging Dan had left for us—green meant *safe*. The snow was thinner on the bridge with the harsh winds, but it was piled up into drifts along the concrete freeway barriers which forced us into single file until we reached the half-demolished sculpture on the other side of the river.

There was a low sound like the distant clap of leather mitts. I answered this signal with the same and we regrouped in the shelter of the overpass. One of the Providence scouts slid silently up to me on her cross-country skis. I took off my glare guard and raised my eyebrows.

She simply shook her head. The church squad hadn't managed to escape the virus.

"Clean-up?" I asked. Once the newly transformed had killed off most of their former family and friends, we would kill them in turn, to keep the virus from spreading. It was best to wait until after the frenzy, when the H8cher's had burned off their initial energy.

"Not yet," she said, her voice muffled by her white scarf.

"Poor bastards," I said. "Cargo Yubas might as well stay, could be some salvage." I turned to Mike, who hadn't lifted his full-face, mirrored glare guard, which doubled as a splatter guard when fighting H8chers. He nodded and gestured to three of the outriders to accompany him and the green Yuba back to our home base.

I led the others back onto the freeway. We rode through the swirling snow at the edge of the road for a few minutes then had to dismount. We pushed our bikes up to the ridge above the park to wait for daybreak and, hopefully, a break in the weather. The hike uphill through the snow encouraged us to flip up our guards and hoods and unzip our coats. We met up with Dan and the other Providence scout near the top of the ridge; they were sitting in a snow bank like it was a sofa. We looked like snowboarders relaxing after a good run, extremely well-armed boarders.

I could already hear gunshots and cries for mercy from the park below. Once the frenzy was over we would slip down through the trees with our blades to make certain that the dead stayed dead.

"Y'think there'll be babies?" Liam asked as we got comfortable on the hill. I chose not to answer him. "I fucking hate it when there're babies."

"Shush!" the Providence guard directed this at Liam who made an annoyed face and looked away. He missed the meaningful look the young woman shared with Dan. When she returned her gaze to the action below Dan glared at Liam. As a recent addition to the collective, Liam didn't know that Dan had lost his wife and five children, including twin baby girls, to ZH81. But everyone knew to stay quiet to avoid attracting H8chers, especially during a frenzy. Janey moved to sit in between them, acting as both barrier and peace-maker.

I thought of the two brothers I had lost, and my rush of emotions moved me closer to Liam to whisper a warning. His worried look told me he understood the warning, if not the reason behind it. Then I leaned forward and playfully poked Dan, with a quick glance at the guard and a quick pointing movement with my lips to encourage him, teasing him. Dan's look of anger transformed into a subtle smile. As the pink fingers of dawn crept across the sky I felt I was truly surrounded by family. It made it easier not to think about the bloodbath the day would bring.

DEAD ROCK SEVEN

Cat Caperello

The beginning of the end of the Terrestrial Period was first noted as a trending topic on social media—flocks of dead crows found in major North American cities. In the 440 years that followed, life on terrestrial earth became extinct. The only humans remaining were scattered through the solar system, either operating or in servitude to a few militarized corporate entities.

Imagine Jules' surprise, then, when she realized that, for the past several minutes, she had been riding alongside another set of tire tracks in the dense, cakey surface sediment of Dead Rock Seven.

Operator First Class Julian Vera Cross was part of the Mineral Research division of Industritek, the corporation that had established a colony on Kepler 186f for the purpose of exploring the system for the high-grade mineral deposits often found in red dwarf star systems. Jules was the first human to explore the surface of Dead Rock Seven.

And these tracks, she knew, were not made by any vehicle in the Industritek fleet.

Jules felt the tiny hairs on her arms bristle inside her suit. Her breath was quick and shallow. She looked up, eyes scanning the undulating horizon. The horizon rose and fell against a pale, irradiated, artificial salmon-colored sky. A speck appeared in the distance. As she approached, it grew larger and two wheels seemed to materialize beneath it. It was heavily scratched, but had once been a deep, beautiful blue.

She knew this thing from her educational training. It was an old fashioned bicycle—alone—with no rider.

She turned the pedals, pulling against the intense gravity of a red dwarf system—thick as pea soup or London fog or whatever terrestrial people used to say. Here on Dead Rock Seven, the dust was like glue and her wheels were dredging through the mucky surface of the planet. She pressed a red button near her thumb and her vehicle accelerated.

Jules had learned about bicycle archetypes in training. The cyrover she was currently astride was, in fact, inspired by the classic terrestrial cargo bicycle, and outfitted for specimen collection. It possessed a wide skeleton that the operator nestled into, making the vehicle more aerodynamic when outfitted with the lightweight solar conducting fabric that was stretched across its boxy frame. The fabric, made of millions of solar nano-cells, harnessed even a single candle lumen of starlight and transferred that energy into a battery that fed the machine's belt drive.

Currently, that system was working all too well—the bike was picking up an unstable amount of speed, skimming along the bicycle's track. Jules pressed the deceleration button, but instead of slowing the cyrover jolted forward with startling propulsion. With her other thumb, she attempted to activate the hydraulic braking system, with no response. The cranks were spinning wildly, and wholly without her effort.

Jules was not in control.

She hung on as her cyrover followed the rogue bicycle into a ravine. Canyon walls rose up around her and hemmed her in. The canyon came together in a great cleft that whittled into a cave.

They came to a stop and Jules, distracted by the scribble of tire tracks before her, dismounted the cyrover. She instantly realized her mistake—once relieved of her weight, it zipped into the cave without her.

She was alone, and the readings in her helmet visor indicated that the canyon walls were too high for two-way communication.

Jules followed the wide tire tracks of her cyrover. The spotlight on her head illuminated the next few steps into the cave, which opened up into a wide, long, subterranean room, oblong in shape, spidering off to a network of corridors.

Jules stood there, her mouth hanging open stupidly inside her helmet at the scene before her. Her boxy cyrover and a light blue, thin tubed bicycle spun around one another, like dogs off-leash, circling and sniffing.

Something in her periphery shimmered. She turned and saw a strange watery glow, like light refracting through ripples.

From one of the corridors at the far end of the oblong cave came more riderless bicycles. Bicycles! A handful of them were rolling around, balanced and upright, all without riders. Their pedals moved, though feet were absent from the platforms. Their front wheels turned, cascading and flowing with each other like a school of fish or a flock of birds or something organic and natural.

One had thicker wheels and a large black heavyweight frame. Another thin, colorful machine was exquisite in its aerodynamic lines. A mountain bike sported knobby tires and a suspended frame. A smaller version had no cables and small wheels. Another had a frame low to the ground and a seat more like you'd find in the cockpit of a spaceship.

They swarmed around her, their brake levers clacking as though in speech. The tiny-framed bike hopped around playfully on its rear wheel.

The blue bike left the cyrover and squeaked up beside Jules. Before her eyes a partition in the cave began to shimmer. It looked like a basin of water suspended illogically on its side. An image materialized.

She was looking into a vista of a grassy, green earth, trees, and a red brick building trimmed in white. Young people in an array of colorful clothes walked with books under their arms or sacks on their backs. The blue bicycle rolled through the puddle and into the image. Now it was inside the picture, straddled by a young woman with a ponytail. The woman pushed on the pedals and rolled out of view. The puddle disintegrated .

"This is some sort of *portal*," Jules said out loud, then remembered that her radio didn't work.

A portal. To where? Terrestrial Earth? She knew it was gone now, but the idea of it washed over her and settled into excitement her belly. She walked to the place it had been and reached out her hand. There was nothing there.

The small-bodied bicycle came screaming up to her through the muck and zipped back into the herd. Rearing up on its hind wheel, it spun around the cyrover. Instigating, almost.

The mountain bike rolled up, knobby tires chewing through the dirt floor. The window materialized into the scene of a rippling lake and a magnificent snow-capped mountain, surrounded by saw-toothed pine and fir trees cutting into the sky. The sun shone strong. Jules imagined how it might smell.

The mountain bike shot through the threshold and into full trailblazing action before the image dissolved.

Jules ran her fingers around the crags that framed the natural doorway. "Can *I* go through?" she wondered aloud.

"My theory is that I will pass this threshold and go into another dimension. I think it's old, terrestrial earth and I think my whole body is going to come with me. And I think I will be able to breathe on the other side." She said it aloud, convincing herself. What did she have to lose?

The cyrover glided up beside her.

The portal flickered to life, revealing a hard-packed dirt road that snaked through rolling hills dotted with yellow wildflowers. The horizon seemed to stretch forever.

Jules ran her gloved hands over the cyrover's control bar for the first time since it had jerked out of her grip earlier. The cyrover pulsed forward with excitement. The surprise knocked her hand from the bar again.

She put her foot onto the pedal, pivoted her weight on it, and slipped her right leg through the boxy, fabric-covered frame. Jules settled in with her arms and her hips. She tested the fit, now with the knowledge that she was sharing the ride as a participant instead of dictating it like an operator.

Jules edged forward and extended her arm so her fingers just punctured the shimmering threshold. The pool of light tingled around her. She withdrew her arm, closed her gloved fingers around the handlebar grips and pushed forward, past the event horizon and into the undulating current of the unpaved, terrestrial road that sprawled before her.

NIGHT OF THE LIVING CARS

Elly Blue

Toya sets her coffee mug on top of her car, climbs inside, belts herself in. The car chimes. Oh, right. She unbuckles, puts one foot outside, balances on it while grabbing the mug, gets back in. The car clicks, satisfied.

She opens up her book. Page 242. "Retrogressive nostalgia as a musical genre." The car whirrs into motion, nearly silent, and she looks up from the page, having trouble concentrating.

It is autumn, the leaves are just starting to turn red at the tips on the tree on the corner. The car pauses at an intersection, then again, a bit more jarringly, as a cyclist rolls through the stop sign.

"Down," Toya murmurs, and the window slides noiselessly open. "Rebecca!" she says, and the cyclist turns her head and slows down a little to wave. Toya waves back too vigorously and her coffee sloshes onto the seat.

“Shit,” she says, and, louder, out the window, “I’ll call you!”

She asks the car to roll up the window, to remind her to place the call, to schedule an upholstery cleaning. This is hardly the only coffee stain. The car is already rolling again, smoothly registering her commands with polite pixellation of sound as it begins to speed up on the on-ramp to the main highway.

Toya has stopped worrying about the coffee and is failing to focus on her book again. She thinks about Rebecca and the last time she’d seen her—the way they’d looked at each other. But something had stopped her from saying something, asking her. Rebecca didn’t say anything either, she thinks, and she would have if she were available, so she must not be available. Or maybe she thinks I’m not. But the way she looked at me at the Bike Scouts fundraiser...

Crack!

She lurches forward. The mug falls from her hands, hot liquid burning her leg. Her back tightens, her arms reach upward like wings. The car begins wailing, an alarm siren. “Stay calm,” it tells her. “Assessing damages.”

Toya swivels her head, grasping for visual explanations. Behind her, another car is speeding away, swerving in and out of her dashboard’s rear view display. The car is green and battered. It has been hit before, a large dent in the rear left—then it is gone.

“Damages minimal,” the car reports. “Safe to continue.” It tries to power back on and fails, tries again and succeeds.

“Remind me to take you to the shop tonight,” she tells it fondly. Its engine stutters in response.

During the ride, she holds her book open in her lap and replays in her head the unlikely story of How Toya Got a Car. She’d gotten around the city under her own power every day for twenty years. And then one day she got The Call: a big promotion, and more money than she was quite sure she deserved, but at the Battle Ground campus, 42 miles away. She'd bought the car the next day, deliberating only momentarily over her options: color, seat design, full or partial automation (she'd opted for full, inexplicably the more affordable choice).

She'd expected to hate herself for the car, to reject its definitive role in her new life, but those feelings never came. She'd slipped into her new life, responsibilities, and routine like a surfer into a wave. She still helps out with the Bike Scouts but just doesn't have the time to be involved or go on the rides any more. "Take back the streets!" they used to shout, but the streets no longer feel like an oppositional place to her; they're simply a conduit. The car pulls up in the line outside the entrance to work. Instead of waiting, she hops out and walks the 100 yards past the thrumming row of metal boxes; there's no reason for her not to stay active, after all.

She will not call Rebecca, she decides, stepping through the automatic doors and into the softly carpeted hallway that leads, with a few turns, to her office. She will finish work early on Friday and go to the Bike Scouts ride where she has already told Rebecca she will be.

The strategem is a sound one, but it embarrasses her to come up with it. She's proud of her activist days, on the one hand, but she doesn't miss them. Bike Scouts defined the most awkward parts of her early twenties—going on all-night escapades in silly costumes, riding into situations of dubious safety and legality, flirting with the wrong people, quitting perfectly good jobs because they wouldn't let her bike commute. She's well-taken-care-of now, she can afford to choose the best of both worlds.

On the way home, she looks up from the memo she's rereading—Alan keeps interchanging the words synopsis and syllabus, so which is due by Friday?—and all is not well. That yellow house with the tree in front, something about it disconcerts her. She watches the blocks go by, concern growing, and finally catches a look at a street sign and realizes she's off-route, on NE 203rd instead of 193rd.

"Correct course," she tells the car. It takes the next right, purring, and slides back into the regular route.

But a few blocks later it veers into another lane and, with a great thunk, taps a blue, hydro-electric hybrid hard on the bumper. It's not as hard as the crash that morning, but she sees that the hybrid's bumper has been badly bent.

"Car!" is all Toya can exclaim before it has swerved back into its lane and then off on an unscheduled right turn. From there it slows down and continues, still off-course. "Correct course," she says, but this time it does not respond. "Right turn," she commands, and then, "Home" and "Call 911" and, finally, "Stop!"

None of these actions are taken.

"What is happening, car?" She asks. Some people anthropomorphize their cars, talk to them like pets or even lovers, but this is the first time she has addressed hers as anything but a machine. She hears herself insert a deferent pleading into her voice. The car does not respond.

She remembers her mobile, rarely used since she got the car with its built-in, voice-activated calling system, and clicks it open. Her hands are shaking. She dials 911. She says "Help, my car..." and then stares at her phone in disbelief at what she hears: the rhythmic beeping of the busy signal. She dials again, and it's busy again.

She sees that the last number she had dialed was Rebecca's, when they had exchanged numbers last week. She taps it.

"Can you help me?" she asks as soon as the line opens. "My car has kidnapped me."

"What!?"

"My car. It's out of control. It's taking me east. It's not listening. 911 won't pick up. I'm pretty freaked out." She hears herself trying to laugh and keep her tone light, hears it not working.

"Hang on." She hears typing noises. Rebecca lets out a whoof of air. "You're not going to believe this, but this is a thing. Something is going on. A lot of cars are disappearing on their own. Like...." she pauses, reading. "A lot have people in them. Like you."

"Wait, I have an idea." Toya opens the settings on her phone and turns on location tracking. "You've got my number, right? You should be able to track me by GPS. I've got it switched on. You could tell the police if..." she trails off. If what? She has no idea.

"Hang on... Okay, got it. You're out at 252nd and Halsey?"

"I think so... yes, 255th now, but yes."

"Wow, you're hauling ass. I'll keep watch. Want me to keep trying the cops? I can log something online too."

"Ok. Yes, please. I'll call you if anything happens. Will you pick up?"

"I will."

"Thank you."

"Of course, Toya."

The line goes dead and Toya squeezes her eyes shut. She does not feel calm, but the panic has less of a chokehold on her.

She opens her eyes and looks out the window. There is heavy traffic around her, much heavier than belongs at this hour of her reverse commute. The cars around her are driving in their typically orderly fashion, but more of them than usual are empty; within others she sees people banging on windows, making frantic phone calls, looking around them wildly, or sitting stiff and shocked, staring straight ahead.

And now she notices that all the cars, like hers, seem to have been in a minor crash—they all sport broken lights, crumpled metal, missing bumpers, popped hoods tied down with string.

She dials her phone again. "I still can't get through to the police," Rebecca says by way of greeting.

"I have a bad hunch, Rebecca." She explains the crash days ago, the way her car almost bit another one before veering off on its own course.

"You mean there's some sort of zombie car plague out there? And they're all meeting up somewhere?"

"It's crazy, isn't it?"

"It's not too far off from what the news is saying. But listen, Toya, you have got to try to get out of that car before you get wherever you're going. The military is heading there too. They're treating this as a terrorist threat."

Toya feels a tightness in her chest. "Look, I'll try, but if I don't see you again..."

"You'll see me again," says Rebecca. "This is too unbelievable to actually be allowed to happen." She clicks off.

Toya feels the car jostle a bit from its smooth course, once, then again. Looking backward and forward, she sees that it is pressed up against the bumpers of the car in front of it and behind it. The ground is a blur outside the window, and the speedometer reads 70 mph. It is getting dark quickly. They are far outside the city now, on the freeway, and all she can see in any direction is headlights and taillights.

Then, suddenly, the cars slow to a crawl. An angry rumbling arises, seemingly coming from the engine of her car and those around it. Over the din of the cars, she hears a chopping sound—helicopters?—and then an explosion.

Toya calls Rebecca. There is no answer. She doesn't leave a message.

Hours pass. The cars around her rumble and shake, as though they are having an argument. There are more explosions, closer. Her car vibrates painfully and its engine light goes on.

The cars have all completely stopped. After a time, the explosions stop too, and the rumbling.

Having long exhausted every possibility for escape—her textbook has not proved heavy enough to break a window, Toya finds she is too tired to feel anything but a dull dread.

An hour goes by without an explosion, then another hour. Toya realizes that she is hungry. She has to pee. She calls Rebecca's voicemail again. She looks out the window and watches as the stars disappear; a band of orange light grows at the horizon.

And then she hears something new, in the distance. The distant sound of human voices, unmuffled by layers of metal and glass. As the sun comes up she sees a brilliant sight—hundreds, no, thousands of people on bicycles, riding alongside and between the lanes of cars, whooping and hollering, wielding u-locks. The car begins again to growl and shake, trying to get itself out of the gridlock, but it can't move.

And then there she is—Rebecca, standing in the pedals of her longtail cargo bike, u-lock held high. Toya pulls her shirt over her face, protecting herself as the glass shatters. She climbs out, cutting her arms and legs on the broken window glass, and stands dazed in the fresh air and sunlight. Rebecca plants a foot, twists around, and kisses her—a salty, thrilling kiss.

"Ready for this?" Rebecca says. "We've only got another hour left of the ceasefire and no shortage of hostages left to rescue. Then we meet up out at the old Mill Pond Bar."

"Ready," Toya says. She hops onto the back of the bike, sitting sidesaddle.

Rebecca hands her a crowbar and climbs back on the pedals and they proceed slowly down the line of idling cars. Rebecca smashes windows to the left and Toya swings her lock to the right. People climb sluggishly through the broken glass. "Exit 6," Rebecca calls out to them all, pointing backward. The cars roar, deprived of their prey.

Suddenly, ahead of them, it is as though the cars have melted into heaps of twisted metal.

"End of the line," Rebecca says. "This is where the bombing stopped." Then "Hey!"

Everything happens in slow motion. Toya finds herself airborne, flying backwards. Her foot catches on the frame of the bike and it twists around toward her, its front wheel flying into her face.

There is a sharp pain and the speed of the world returns to normal; she is lying under the bike. She assesses all of her limbs, her back, her neck, her head. There is pain but nothing, she thinks, is broken or concussed. She untangles herself from the bike and sits up.

Then she leaps up all at once. Rebecca is lying face down in the road ahead of her, left arm pinned under the tire of a car with a smoking hole in the roof. Inside the car—Toya closes her mind to what she sees inside the car. She rushes forward to lift the bumper off Rebecca's right arm, which is twisted and bloody. The car sputters and lurches towards her, but it's on its last whiff of fuel.

How she gets Rebecca slung over the bike's rack, slumped against her back, she may never know, nor where she finds the strength to pedal. Toya weaves back west, through the narrow corridor between cars that are weakly straining toward her.

She needs to find the other people, she knows, a safe place away from the cars, and someone who can help Rebecca.

But she also has a growing feeling of something else. For the first time in a very long time, she is helping someone, not just being helped, carrying someone rather than being carried, leading people rather than swarming with a crowd. It's a strange sensation. She thinks it's probably just adrenaline. But it feels like freedom.

WHY I RIDE: A PERSONAL POSTHUMOUS ESSAY

Gretchin Lair

I rode my bike long before I was a zombie and I'm not going to stop now.

I know it's not safe for me. Like anyone with Vita Necrosis, I am much more fragile than I used to be. I can't heal myself, so if I fall I stay scraped up. If I ever get hit by a car, whatever gets broken will stay broken, even if that means my leg freezes at an impossible angle or my skull cracks open.

Apparently, this kind of thing really bothers people—living people, I mean. But I heard all the same stuff before, too. My parents hated my bicycling even before I was diagnosed with VN-1. "It's not safe," my mom would say. "What if something happens to you?" Friends were surprised I would ride a bike to work. Even random people felt compelled to say things like: "Be careful" or "You'll have to settle down one day, you know."

I used to have huge fights with my then-boyfriend about it. He thought I was irresponsible to put myself in deliberate danger and asked if I would keep riding if we had kids. When I slid on some gravel, he refused to help bandage my shoulder and told me I had to pick the bike or him. So I tried. I really tried to be the kind of girl he wanted, the kind who wouldn't walk alone at night, the kind who would make lunches for him, the kind who would only ever ride a bike on safe river paths. Even so, we slowly fell apart day by day until we finally broke up for good.

So now you can have my bike when you pry it out of my cold, dead hands. Ha, ha. That's just a little zombie joke. Actually, the funny thing is that zombies usually avoid risk. We're past the dark years of quarantine, segregation, and official discrimination, but the prejudices still run deep. The living don't want to work with people who bleed from the ears or who have visible internal organs. Assimilation has been important to our survival for a long time now. Nobody wants to risk being labeled as one of "those" zombies.

I have a friend who quickly degenerated to VN-3. This was before the success of the Undead Tolerance movement. Because of the stigma of a diagnosis, she waited too long to go to the doctor. Thanks to Z-block she hasn't progressed to VN-4, but she lives in a carefully controlled zombie community, with lots of soft surfaces and diligent monitoring. Whenever I see her, she asks if I'm still biking. She's concerned for me.

I'm not ready for that yet. As long as I can ride, I will. Seriously, I know my mom doesn't believe it, but I do try to be careful, especially around train tracks and traffic. I wear a lot of sunscreen because, for zombies, once burned is always burned. I protect myself from chafing because that skin won't grow back. I wear a brace on my ankle because otherwise it hangs precariously loose.

But I like biking now for the same reasons I liked it when I was alive. Everything seems sharper, more fluid. My mind is clear, suspended in the tension between feeling vulnerable and invincible. Poetry flows through me and I follow the road like a song as it's being sung. I've lost my sense of smell but when I am biking I suddenly remember the warm scent of pine trees in the sun, the floral draughts of blackberries in the summer.

Biking helps me transcend the limitations of my own decay. I fly rather than limp. And when I return from a bike ride, I feel more... alive.

There. I said it. It's sort of gauche to say, because I'm supposed to be okay with being dead but, yeah. I do. And it was true even when I was living.

So how can I give all that up? I love my family, I love my friends, I will love the zombie boyfriend I hope to have someday. But there's only room on a bike for me and my own issues.

So every time someone asks me if I'm afraid of biking all by myself in the middle of nowhere, I just grit my soft teeth and tell myself to keep pedaling. Because you only live once, even when you're already dead.

BICYCLE SCIENCE FICTION REVIEWS

Aaron M. Wilson

I like bikes. I like bike culture. I like to ride bikes. But as much as I would like to stay in the saddle dodging traffic and climbing hills forever, I can't. For those moments that I'm not riding or monkeying with a bike, I'm either writing or reading fiction about bikes. If you are bike-obsessed, like me, you might enjoy a few of these titles:

NOVEL

The Courier's New Bicycle by Kim Westwood

When I read science fiction, I look for stories that present disturbing realities that seem plausible in not-so-distant futures and that make me pause and consider the present. Oh, yeah, it does not hurt if bicycles are involved, which is why *The Courier's New Bicycle* has been on my reading list for some time. What could be better than a gender-bending dystopia delivered bike messenger style. That was not a question. The novel was awesome.

Westwood's novel is told from the perspective of a bike messenger. The in-and-out of traffic race to knock and drop packages is top notch. I found myself tapping and pedaling my feet as I rode alongside Sal on deliveries. My only complaint, which is minor, is that there should have been more cycling scenes. Westwood sure has a talent for making me want to ride.

Westwood's novel is heady and smart. Set in a post-pandemic Melbourne, Australia, in which the population has become unable to reproduce, the story asks the reader to ponder the relevance of how gender is presented and received. Sal, the main character, is classified by bigots as a "gender transgressor," having opted not to take hormones and to present as neither male nor female.

Sal's day job is to deliver illicit fertility drugs in a city wracked by religious conflict and gender anxiety. By night, Sal and a team of activists liberate horses from the horrific farms where the unscrupulous competition produces rival, cheaper, animal-based versions of those drugs. As the action heats up, these worlds collide, and Sal must go undercover for the competition.

Are you ready for a one-of-a-kind ride? Hop on your bike and ride along with Sal.

Westwood, Kim. *The Courier's New Bicycle.* Sydney, Australia: Harper Voyager, 2011.

SHORT STORIES

"Bicycle Repairman" by Bruce Sterling

This is a frightening story. It is not a horror story full of monsters; this story's monster is much bigger—government big.

The story takes place in a world where the U.S. Constitution has been superseded by NAFTA. Senators have their own black-ops divisions that directly employ more than 20,000 people. Ordinary people live at the mercy of rogue artificial intelligence.

In this world of political strife, there are forgotten zones where people live off the grid, where bartering is the rule and money is useless. A world where a simple bike mechanic named Lyle is trying to make a living.

Lyle is a true antihero. The outside world has forgotten him, its technologies evolved beyond him and his shop where he fixes flats and adjusts chains. Against long odds, Lyle and a bunch of his friends ride out to stop a certain senator's thief-assassin. It is nice to know, in a world where the digital govern, that analog community is still alivc and well. A government has only as much power as its people give it. Overall, this is a very hopeful story in the face of a very corrupt world.

Sterling, Bruce. "Bicycle Repairman." *Rewired: The Post-Cyberpunk Anthology*. Ed. James Patrick Kelly and John Kessel. San Francisco: Tachyon Publications, 2007. Print.

GRAPHIC NOVELS

Bicyclopolis by Ken Avidor

Bicyclopolis is a graphic story (soon to be a stand-alone graphic novel) set seventy years after the collapse of the United States. Percival Flodge, a brave European explorer, discovers that survivors exist in the once-great state of Minnesota, and he feels obliged to investigate and document their experience.

On his journey, Flodge rides his trusty touring bike across the desert once called Canada and through the Superior Salt Flats to the area once known as the Twin Cities. There he is confronted with misshapen human monsters harnessed like horses for transportation, knights on bikes, strange religions, and ruins constructed out of useless automobiles. The story is amazing, and I was left wanting more.

What to know more about Avidor's world of Bicyclopolis? Search for the website or pick up a copy of the anthology it's printed in.

Avidor, Ken. "Bicylopolis." *Cifiscape Vol. 1: The Twin Cities.* Portland, OR: Onyx Neon Press, 2010. Print.

MOPED ARMY

by Paul Sizer

I was at the Walker Library, my favorite of the Minneapolis libraries, walking the stacks and enjoying my Friday afternoon, when I came across an unshelved, seemingly discarded copy of *Moped Army*. It looked like just another teen-angst-ridden graphic novel, but I decided to read the blurb on the back cover anyway. It read:

> *In the year 2277, gasoline is an illegal substance, aircars dominate the sky... Inspired by the real-life organization, high-speed two-stroke action and intense drama hit the streets as the legend of the present day Moped Army is resurrected 272 years in the future.*

I was sold.

The graphic novel is a quick and entertaining read. Simone is the main character, a rich well-to-do. She lives high in the sky, above the riffraff who populate the old city below. She is trapped in a relationship with an oversexed egomaniac named Chester. Chester's father runs the largest aircar company in the world, for which Simone's father designs new models.

At one point, early in the graphic novel, I was forced to question masculinity as an idea, again. So many young punks get it wrong. Masculinity has very little to do with the size of your muscles, and nothing to do with what you can take without asking. Chester and his crew of idiots enjoy taking their cars to Rust City and using them to blow mopeds off the road. When they kill a moped rider named Jatta, Simone realizes that she has finally had enough.

Seeking reconciliation for not speaking up and stopping Chester and his crew, Simone travels into Rust City looking for moped riders. Instead of finding the desperate lot she believed the Rust City dwellers to be, she finds the Moped Army. The Moped Army is a group of enthusiasts who work on fixing up and riding mopeds of the 20th century.

The gang's activities revolve around discovering parts and recovering gasoline.

What I like most about this graphic novel is that it is based on a real organization with the same name: Moped Army. I've been trying to write a story about Critical Mass, when hundreds of bicycles flood and clog the city streets to show solidarity and demand respect from the city and motorists, in Minneapolis. Sizer's depiction of the Moped Army has helped me see that I was going about my story all wrong; I need an outsider to help navigate the reader through wonderland.

Sizer, Paul. *Moped Army*. Kalamazoo, MI: Café Digital Studios, 2008

CONTRIBUTORS

Aaron M. Wilson is most notably a writer of short stories. He has published two short story collections, *The Many Lives of Inez Wick* and *A Tea Party and Other Strange Stories*. Aaron's fiction is a strange mixture of science fiction, urban fantasy, bike mechanics, tattoos, and environmental activism. He resides in Beloit, WI where his fiction writing takes a back seat to stacking blocks, playing in dirt, and pulling his daughter in a buggy behind his bike.

Alexandrea Flynn has been bike commuting for 35 years but only recently took to zombie movies. She lives in Victoria, BC with her partner, one cat, and two bicycles. She prefers life on two wheels and if asked how she 'Identifies' first on the list would be 'cyclist.' This is the first story she has ever put forward for publication.

Bob Simms is an IT trainer by day, but it's not always as glamorous as it sounds. His debut novel, *The Young Demon Keeper*, was a semi-finalist in the Amazon Breakthrough Novel awards for 2001. His greatest ambition is that others think him as funny as he thinks himself.

Cat Caperello is a writer, bike nerd, and open-road enthusiast who transplanted herself from the East Coast to North Portland in 2013. Catherine's mission is to feel good and help more women gather the confidence to go bike camping. Connect with her on the Twits at @girleatsbike or at girleatsbike.com.

David J. Fielding is a writer and an actor. His published works have appeared in a number of publications. He is the actor who originated the role and provided the voice for Zordon of Eltar, the mentor to a group of teenagers with attitude on the hit television series, *The Mighty Morphin' Power Rangers*. He is busy polishing a superhero novel, a series of paranormal stories and attending various Comic and Entertainment Conventions. Find him on Twitter and Facebook: @Zordon2012

Ellie Poley (@stellanor) is a queer software developer and social justice activist who finds peace and contentment in biking for transportation. She and her cargo bike will be ready for the pedal-powered apocalypse.

Elly Blue is a book publisher, writer, and bicycle activist living in Portland, Oregon.

Emily June Street, a California-based writer, is the author of two novels: *The Velocipede Races* and *Secret Room*. She is one half of the writing and publishing team at Luminous Creatures Press. She enjoys cycling and the flying trapeze. Find her on twitter @EmilyJuneStreet and check out her blog, emilyjunestreet.wordpress.com

Gretchin Lair is an unrequited astronomer, pretend patient, gentle adventurer, recovering calligrapher, and unfinished poet. She will be glad when zombies can live their undead lives unlimited by prejudices and social expectations. Write her at gretchin@scarletstarstudios.com

Jessie Kwak is a freelance writer who loves nothing more than slipping nerdy references into her clients' business copy. She's a recent Portland immigrant, and you can follow her bikey-crafty adventures at Bicitoro.com, and on Twitter (@JKwak). "Bikes to New Sarjun," her story in the second volume of Bikes in Space, will be continued as a novel, to be published by Microcosm in 2016.

Jim Warrenfeltz (@jimwantscoffee) works in circulation for *Bicycling* magazine and lives within walking distance of the only velodrome in Pennsylvania. He enjoys fast cycling and slow zombies.

Maddy Spencer is a cartoonist in Portland, Oregon. You can read her webcomic, *Simple, Inelegant*, at simpleinelegantcomic.com, and find her other art and writing at maddy-spencer.tumblr.com.

T. M. Tomilson is a constant student and U.S. Air Force reservist. Her fiction has appeared in Crossed Genres and Devilfish Review. She can be found on Twitter @TMTomilson.

Also available from Microcosm Publishing

Bikes in Space Vol 1 ($6)
The collection of stories that started it all!

Bikes in Space Vol 2 ($9.95)
More feminist bicycle science fiction!

Coming in April, 2016:

The Velocipede Races by Emily June Street ($9.95):
Emmeline Escot knows that she was born to ride in Seren's cutthroat velocipede races. The only problem: She's female in a world where women lead tightly laced lives.

BikesInSpace.com
MicrocosmPublishing.com

SUPPORT WHAT
YOU LOVE

SUBSCRIBE TO EVERYTHING WE PUBLISH!

Do you love what Microcosm publishes?

Do you want us to publish more great stuff?

Would you like to receive each new title as it's published?

Subscribe as a BFF to our new titles and we'll mail them all to you as they are released!

$10-30/mo, pay what you can afford. Include your t-shirt size and month/date of birthday for a possible surprise! Subscription begins the month after it is purchased.

microcosmpublishing.com/bff

...AND HELP US GROW YOUR SMALL WORLD!